I LOVE THE MOUNTAINS

Retold by STEVEN ANDERSON

Illustrated by ANNIE WILKINSON

CANTATA
LEARNING

WWW.CANTATALEARNING.COM

CANTATA LEARNING

Published by Cantata Learning
1710 Roe Crest Drive
North Mankato, MN 56003
www.cantatalearning.com

Library of Congress Control Number: 2015932804
Anderson, Steven.
    I Love the Mountains / retold by Steven Anderson; Illustrated by Annie Wilkinson
    Series: Sing-along Science Songs
    Audience: Ages: 3–8; Grades: PreK–3
    Summary: Have you ever seen a mountain? In this classic song, you're invited to
join a little girl and her father as they spend time hiking and camping in the mountains
while being serenaded by all sorts of woodland animal friends.
    ISBN: 978-1-63290-376-1 (library binding/CD)
    ISBN: 978-1-63290-507-9 (paperback/CD)
    ISBN: 978-1-63290-537-6 (paperback)
    1. Stories in rhyme. 2. Mountains—fiction.

Book design, Tim Palin Creative
Editorial direction, Flat Sole Studio
Music direction, Elizabeth Draper
Music arranged and produced by Mark Oblinger

Printed in the United States of America in North Mankato, Minnesota.
122015   0326CGS16

ACCESS THE MUSIC!

SCAN CODE WITH MOBILE APP

CANTATALEARNING.COM

The mountains can be a **peaceful**, happy place. In the mountains, you will see plants, animals, and beautiful **scenery**.

Now turn the page and sing about the mountains!

I love the mountains.
I love the rolling hills.

I love the flowers.

I love the **daffodils**.

I love the tall peaks.
I love the icy snow.

I love the **fireside**
when all the lights are low.

9

We walk together,
hiking by the quiet stream.

We watch for the sunrise,
breathing the air so clean.

When we're together,
sharing our **fondest** dreams.

Boom dee ah dah. Boom dee ah dah.

Boom dee ah dah. Boom dee ah dah.

I love the mountains.
I love the rolling hills.

16

I love the flowers.
I love the daffodils.

17

I love the tall peaks.
I love the icy snow.

I love the fireside
when all the lights are low.

SONG LYRICS
I Love the Mountains

I love the mountains.
I love the rolling hills.

I love the flowers.
I love the daffodils.

I love the tall peaks.
I love the icy snow.

I love the fireside
when all the lights are low.

Boom dee ah dah. Boom dee ah dah.
Boom dee ah dah. Boom dee ah dah.
Boom dee ah dah. Boom dee ah dah.
Boom dee ah dah. Boom dee ah dah.

We walk together,
hiking by the quiet stream.

We watch for the sunrise,
breathing the air so clean.

When we're together,
sharing our fondest dreams.

Boom dee ah dah. Boom dee ah dah.
Boom dee ah dah. Boom dee ah dah.
Boom dee ah dah. Boom dee ah dah.
Boom dee ah dah. Boom dee ah dah.

I love the mountains.
I love the rolling hills.

I love the flowers.
I love the daffodils.

I love the tall peaks.
I love the icy snow.

I love the fireside
when all the lights are low.

Boom dee ah dah. Boom dee ah dah.
Boom dee ah dah. Boom dee ah dah.
Boom dee ah dah. Boom dee ah dah.
Boom dee ah dah. Boom dee ah dah.

I Love the Mountains

World
Mark Oblinger

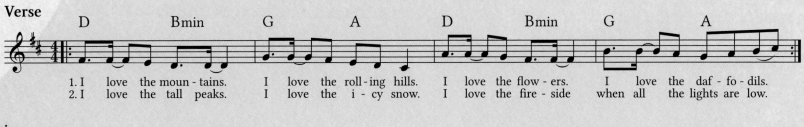

Verse

1. I love the mountains. I love the rolling hills. I love the flowers. I love the daffodils.
2. I love the tall peaks. I love the icy snow. I love the fireside when all the lights are low.

Refrain　　　　　　　　　　　　　　　　　　　　　　　　　　　　　　　　　　**Fine**

Boom dee ah dah. Boom dee ah dah.　　　　　Boom dee ah dah. Boom dee ah dah.

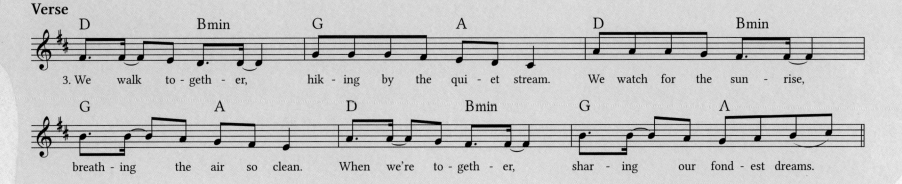

Verse

3. We walk together, hiking by the quiet stream. We watch for the sunrise, breathing the air so clean. When we're together, sharing our fondest dreams.

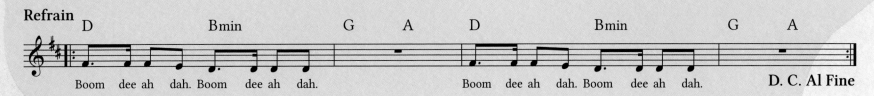

Refrain

Boom dee ah dah. Boom dee ah dah.　　　　　Boom dee ah dah. Boom dee ah dah.

D. C. Al Fine

23

GLOSSARY

daffodils—a kind of flower

fireside—a place near a fire

fondest—happiest or most loving

peaceful—calm and quiet

scenery—the view of one's surroundings

GUIDED READING ACTIVITIES

1. This story takes place in the mountains. Have you ever seen a mountain? What was it like?

2. The girl and her father share their "fondest" dreams. What do you think their dreams are? What dreams do you have?

3. Draw some daffodils and other beautiful flowers until you have a whole garden.

TO LEARN MORE

Anderson, Sheila. *What Can Live in the Mountains?* Minneapolis, MN: Lerner, 2010.

Hutmacher, Kimberly M. *Mountains.* North Mankato, MN: Capstone Press, 2011.

Labrecque, Ellen. *Living on a Mountain.* North Mankato, MN: Heinemann-Raintree, 2015.

Underwood, Deborah. *Hiding in Mountains.* North Mankato, MN: Heinemann-Raintree, 2011.